I WENT TO THE SUPERMARKET

Paul Howard

BLOOMSBURY

LONDON OXFORD NEW YORK NEW DELHI SYDNEY

For Tiggy

Bloomsbury Publishing, London, New Delhi, New York and Sydney

First published in Great Britain in 2016 by Bloomsbury Publishing Plc
50 Bedford Square, London, WC1B 3DP

Text and illustrations copyright © Paul Howard 2016
The moral right of the author/illustrator has been asserted

A CIP catalogue record for this book is available from the British Library

ISBN 978 1 4088 4468 7 (HB)
ISBN 978 1 4088 4470 0 (PB)
ISBN 978 1 4088 4469 4 (eBook)

Printed in China by Leo Paper Products, Heshan, Guangdong

1 3 5 7 9 10 8 6 4 2

www.bloomsbury.com

All papers used by Bloomsbury Publishing are natural, recyclable products
made from wood grown in well-managed forests.
The manufacturing processes conform to the environmental regulations of the country of origin

BLOOMSBURY is a registered trademark of Bloomsbury Publishing Plc

I went to the **supermarket** and I bought...

a pair
of
superhero
pants.

Well...

I went to the

supermarket

and I bought a pair

of superhero **pants**

and...

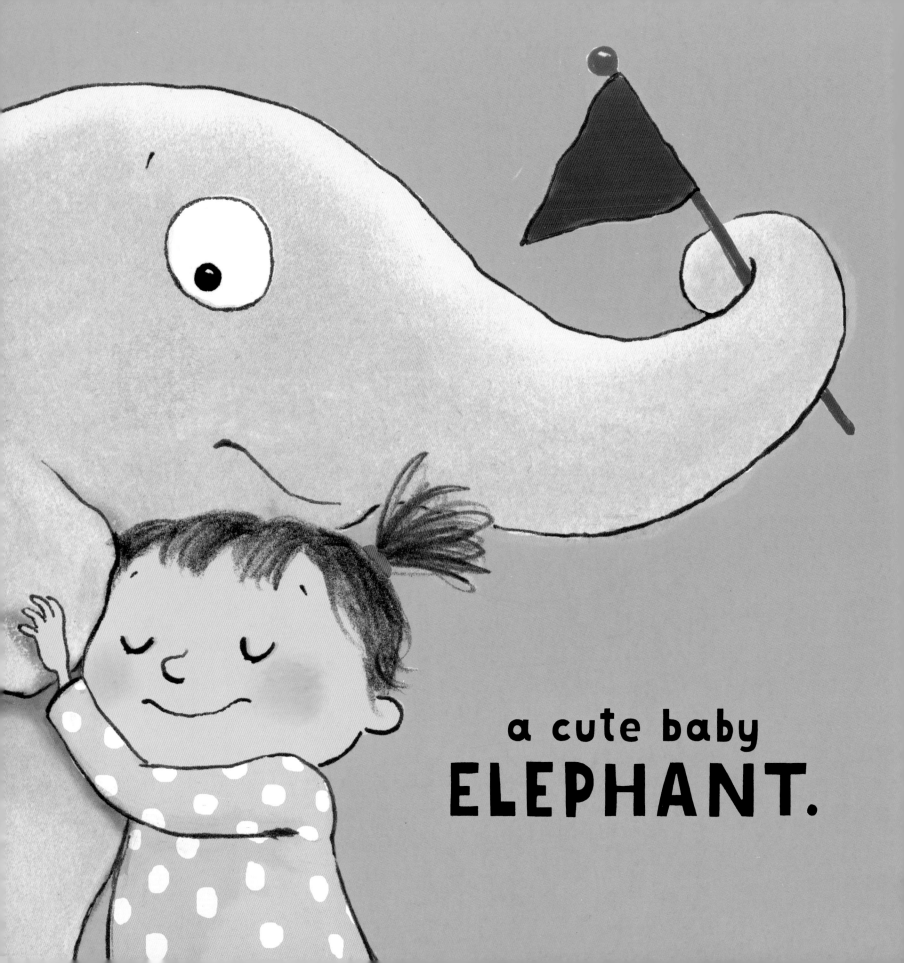

a cute baby
ELEPHANT.

I went to the

supermarket

and I bought a pair
of superhero pants,
a cute baby ELEPHANT
and . . .

Well I went to the **supermarket** and I bought a pair of superhero **pants**, a cute baby ELEPHANT, a **tuba**

and . . .

a fearsome
granny
PIRATE!

I went to the **supermarket** and I bought a pair of superhero **pants,**

a cute **baby ELEPHANT,** a **tuba,** a fearsome granny pirate **and some...**

dancing **A L I**

E N S.

Well I went to the **supermarket** and I bought a pair of superhero **pants,** a cute baby **ELEPHANT,** a **tuba,**

a fearsome granny pirate, some dancing **ALIENS** and . . .

a fire-breathing DRAGON!

I went to the **supermarket** and I bought a pair of superhero **pants**, a cute baby **ELEPHANT**, a **tuba**, a fearsome granny pirate, some dancing **ALIENS**, a fire-breathing **DRAGON** and...

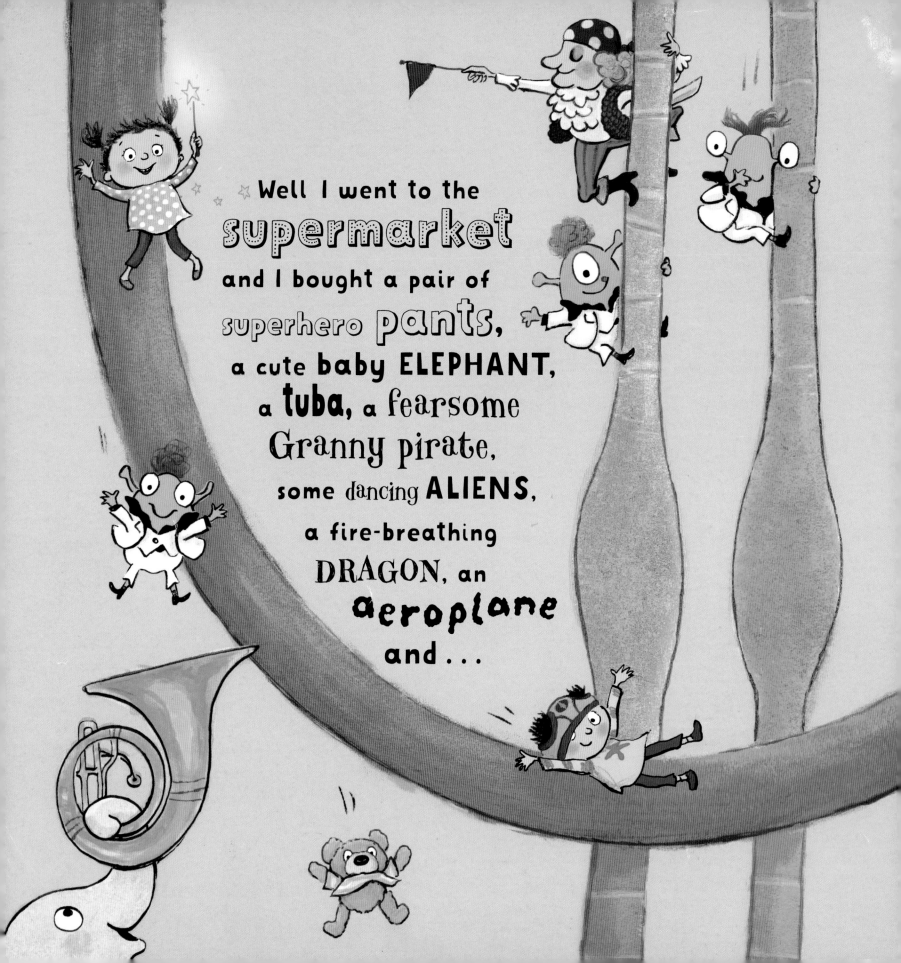

Well I went to the
supermarket
and I bought a pair of
superhero **pants**,
a cute **baby ELEPHANT**,
a **tuba**, a fearsome
Granny pirate,
some dancing **ALIENS**,
a fire-breathing
DRAGON, an
aeroplane
and . . .

a giant pink
FLAMINGO!

I went to the **supermarket** and I bought a pair of superhero **pants**, a cute **baby ELEPHANT**, a **tuba**, a fearsome granny pirate, some dancing **ALIENS**, a fire-breathing **DRAGON**, an **aeroplane**, a giant pink **FLAMINGO** and...

a mountain of **Jelly!**

Well I went to the **supermarket** and I bought a pair of superhero **pants**, a cute baby **ELEPHANT**, a **tuba**, a fearsome granny pirate,

some dancing **ALIENS**, a fire-breathing **DRAGON**, an **aeroplane**, a giant pink **FLAMINGO**, a mountain of **Jelly** and . . .

I went to the
supermarket
and I bought....
a pair of
superhero **pants**,

a cute baby
ELEPHANT,

a **tuba,**

PoP

some dancing **ALIENS** . . .

POP

POP

POP

a fearsome granny **pirate,**

a fire-breathing DRAGON,

an aeroplane,

POP

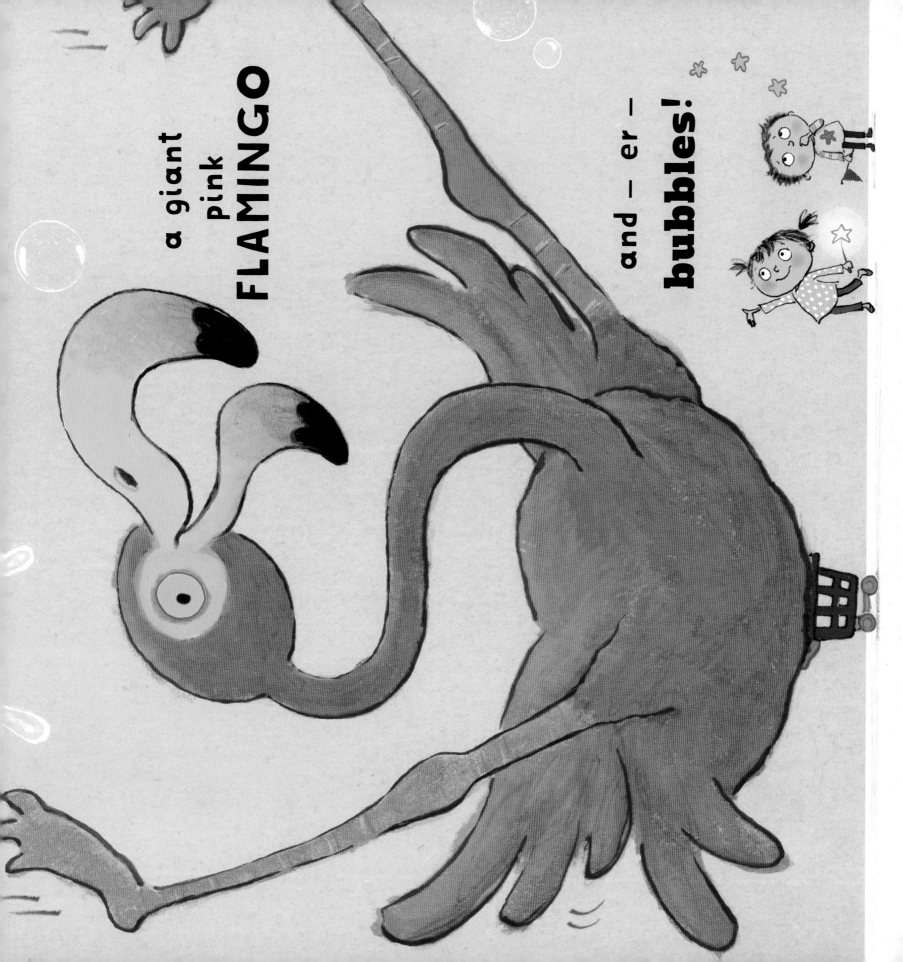

a giant pink **FLAMINGO**

and — er — **bubbles!**

POP

Ha! Ha! I win.
You forgot something.

Did I?
What was it?

a pair of
superhero **pants,**

a cute baby
ELEPHANT,

a **tuba,**

a fearsome
granny pirate,

some dancing
ALIENS,

a fire-breathing
DRAGON,

an aeroplane,

a giant pink
FLAMINGO,

bubbles and . . . and . . . and . . .

splat!

Oh, yes it was
the **Jelly!**
Silly me . . .
I win!